I0652127

Anhedonia

A Collection of Short
Stories by

Ted McLoof

Finishing Line Press
Georgetown, Kentucky

Anhedonia

ACKNOWLEDGMENTS

"Space, Whether, and Why" in *Monkeybicycle*, August 2011
"Host" in *Juked*, March 2014
"Disneyland" in *Gertrude*, February 2011
"Home Sweet Home" in *DIAGRAM*, summer 2013
"Anhedonia" in *Kenyon Review*, summer 2014
"How to Start Again in Twelve Easy Steps" in Associative Press,
        summer 2013
"Negotiation" in *Louisville Review*, spring 2014

The author would like to thank the following: his wife, Sydney, for her
unwavering support and love; Honey, for being a catalyst for the whole
collection; Grant Faulkner, for being an early champion of these pieces and
giving them a much needed boost; Manuel Munoz and Benjamin Rybeck
for reading these stories, and listening to the real-life situations that inspired
to them, ad nauseum; and to Eric Sandve, in loving memory, my forever
brother in story-swapping. Rest in peace, my friend.

Publisher: Leah Huete de Maines
Editor: Christen Kincaid
Cover Art and Design: Jonathan Robert Harmon
Author Photo: Allison Holstrom

Order online: www.finishinglinepress.com
        also available on amazon.com

Author inquiries and mail orders:
Finishing Line Press
P. O. Box 1626
Georgetown, Kentucky 40324
U. S. A.

Table of Contents

I'm not sayin' you treated me unkind
You coulda done better, but I don't mind
You just kinda wasted my precious time.
But don't think twice—it's alright.

—Bob Dylan

1. Space, Whether, and Why

Space, Whether, and Why.

You liked to talk, and so did I, but we always spoke in different ways: I am from the East Coast and liked to talk about the people I loved and the places I was attached to, but you are from the West Coast and liked to talk about *whether* I loved those people or *why* I was so attached, and I thought *man this is a chick you could learn a few things from*, and so we started to speak in these terms, we started to question the merits of all the things I adored, and I didn't for one second find it presumptuous because you seemed to know your shit: I told you that Vivian had broken my heart because I loved her so, so much, loved her in a way I didn't think I could love someone, and you said *how long did you date* and I said *three months* and you looked at me as though I'd just revealed that Vivian was actually a guy or something, and then we talked about *why* it was wrong to love her, and *why* it was wrong to even call it love at all, and why I had to cut it out, and then you told me you needed "space," but I'm from the East Coast and had never heard that word before, not in the way you were using it, not phrased as a thing you request of someone you love very much, but you are from the West Coast and said that your therapist had taught you to use this word openly and often, to ask for it at will, this therapist who had also taught you the language of *whether* and *why*, and so "space" it was: we stopped lying all afternoon together in your studio with the high white walls and the large stone tiles and the French press and the Ikea bed that I built for you when you moved in; we stopped dancing to Al Green at two in the afternoon when we were supposed to be in class learning about the Art of the Memoir; we stopped taking walks around your stone-cobbled neighborhood, and wondering who lived in each house, and making up stories about their lives—we stopped doing all of this because you needed "space," and when I asked you what you needed "space" for, as in *what is it you do when you're taking your "space"* rather than *what kind of a person asks for "space"*, in other words out of genuine curiosity instead of a kind of accusation, you stood barefoot in the kitchen and rubbed your big toe against your calf like a flamingo, and I loved you so, so much, loved you in a way I didn't think I could love someone, loved you in a way I hadn't even loved Vivian, loved you in a way that made me want the *opposite* of "space," in a way that wasn't even physically possible, wanted to figure out how we could just dissolve into each other or melt or whatever, because I could tell you were nervous, and you never let anyone see when you were nervous, but you were letting me see, and then you said *I'm confused* and

I said *what about* and you tied your hair back in a ponytail and put your foot down and said *I've been talking to some of my ex-boyfriends lately*, and when I paused for a breath, you rolled your eyes and said *you need to find a way to deal with your anger*, because I am from the East Coast and called your ex-boyfriend a dickhead, or something like that, because he once shouted to a passing car that he was going to quote ride you all night long unquote, and I couldn't imagine you ever dating a person who'd say that, and you are from the West Coast and so said *well, let's talk about why you're having trouble accepting that*, and I said *okay*, and we talked about what was "really" the matter, and I'm from the East Coast so I said *you're selfish*, and you're from the West Coast and said *sometimes in love you need to be selfish*, and I could see you getting impatient and so I agreed, and then you went home for summer and we decided it would be fun to write each other letters, like an old-fashioned couple, instead of using the phone, and over three months apart I sent two a week, and you sent one a month, each letter becoming sparser in content and more clinical in tone, which was something I probably would have been able to detect sooner had I not skipped so many craft classes with you, and you came back and told me about the men you'd been with, and when I cried you said *well let's talk about why this is hurting you so much*, and I managed to talk through the tears but every time we got to the part where we described what you'd done, I hit the dashboard (we were in your car in front of my apartment) with my palm, and you said *see what I mean? You always turn to anger*, and I said *I'm sorry* and I said *you're right* because you were getting impatient, and ready to let me out of the car, and you said *okay let's just see what happens*, and we continued on like that: we got drunk with our friends and made love afterward when you said *say it again, say the thing you wanted* and I said *I want to dissolve into you*, and you liked that, and I liked that you liked that, because I meant it, even while drunk, and things were back on track until Halloween, when we found the dog wandering in front of the car, and we took her to a shelter but they were closed, and by then I could see by the look in your eyes that you were already in love, but your roommate had cats and so we kept the dog at my house, and called her Honey because "Wild Honey" by the Beach Boys had been playing on the radio when we found her, and she was a beautiful dog, but frightened easily during sleep, and so you started sleeping at your place, and we had conversations about What It Means to Have a Dog Together, which always ended with you saying it's not something you were interested in doing, not with me, and you are from the West Coast and said *I've decided I can't take her, it's too stressful for me*, and when I asked which rescue place we should take her to, you said *why can't you just take her in? Please?* and we had a conversation about what was wrong with me and why I couldn't handle the responsibility—I had no money but you said *if you love something enough you'll find a way*, and I am from the East Coast so I looked at you, and agreed, and took her in, and I did end up loving her so, so much, loved her in a way I didn't think I could love a dog, loved her like a father loves a daughter, and then you went home for Christmas, and didn't come back, and called me and told me about the men you'd been with *this* time, and said *you need to find a way to deal with your anger*, and said *I need space*, and I gave it to you, and now here I am with Honey, Honey who I love, Honey who is all I have left of you, and I think about how much I love her, and I think about the "value" of "space," because that's how you've taught me to think, and I try to picture ever wanting "space" from this thing that I love so much, and I can't picture ever asking that of something I love, and I think about how I'd never allow her that kind of "space" if she really was my daughter and had the ability to request it, how I'd simply say *no space between us*, and as I lie here with her I think about *why* you knew everything, and *whether* you ever really knew anything.

———

2. Disneyland

Disneyland.

When I was sixteen I still hadn't grown breasts, but I had already fallen in love for the first time. Beneath that small chest beat a heart to be reckoned with, and Penny, the girl I'd fallen for, was hell-bent on doing just that. We didn't do much—just made out in my car a few times, in the school parking lot at night so that no one would know. She told me a thousand times if she told me once that she wasn't a lesbian, she didn't know what the hell she was doing really. She broke my heart, and I was convinced that this would be my fate: I would be facing an entire lifetime of pain like this, and no one would ever love me. These were the thoughts I had when I was sixteen. It was that kind of heartbreak, and I was that kind of sixteen-year-old.

All this is to say that I never normally would have asked my father for advice. I hadn't before and I haven't since. But the timing was right: not only had I just been hurt, but this was also two years after my mother kicked him out, and he was pretty dutifully trying to rebuild his life. During my once-a-month visit to his walk-up apartment, with its steel, paint-peeled door and its fifteen locks, I decided to take a gamble. He had just come back from a run and still had his red-white-and-blue sweatband on, was still wearing his torn Umbro shorts, red-faced with beads of sweat pooling at his temples. I took a chance and asked him, Dad, if you could offer me any sort of advice about women, what would it be?

You had to be frank with dad. He didn't like to beat around the bush and when you did he pretended not to understand your point. This was how my mother usually spoke to him, at least. She told me this was how you had to speak to men. I learned a lot about men and women in those years, during the battle of the exes. I actually don't know if I'd told him I was gay before then. That sounds weird, but Dad was like that. Conversations with him were like cat-doors: subjects sort of wandered in and out at their own free will, and you never knew whether they'd left the house for good or whether they'd come back, mysteriously, five pounds fatter.

In any case, he didn't seem all that surprised, and it didn't occur to me at the time how odd his response was; he didn't shut his eyes or pause for a beat or even stroke his goatee as he often did when he was thinking deeply. Instead he just sat down on the chair—with no concern whatsoever for the stain his sweaty shorts might leave on the seat, odd for him—across from me, wiped his forearm across his face, put a hand on my shoulder, and spoke:

"Lynn. There's not a lot I can tell you about women. I'm only good for them for a short time. I'm very much like milk in that way. Milk isn't a necessity, but it always seems like one when you're about to buy it, and it's good at first, but it has a very specific expiration date. Just a few weeks. After that it's no good anymore. Actually, never mind, Lynn. Ignore that. That's a terrible metaphor."

He didn't mean metaphor. He meant simile, but I got what he was going for. He paid for two-thirds of my SAT classes because he never went to college himself and thought I "had something." I didn't like pointing that out, though, so I didn't bother correcting him.

"Here's what I'm like, I think: Disneyland. That makes more sense, because milk is at least practical, and there's an infinite supply of it, and what good it did you is gone after it expires. It changes, is what I'm saying I guess, in reality and not just in the mind of whoever buys it. Disneyland, though. That makes more sense."
I was supposed to be going to a friend's party that night and I glanced quickly at the clock to see how much time I'd have to get ready. There would be girls there.

"I'm very good for women for a one-month stretch. I'll bring them flowers, and I'll write them notes, and I'll tell them I love them and that I need them and that I can't picture my life without them and all of the other silly things people say to each other when they're falling in love. Women need this sometimes, to recharge their batteries, to let them know that they're worthy of being loved."

I told him that made sense, and that I didn't understand: why just a month?

"People work their entire lives. Work kills them, it wears them down. They like to take trips for this reason: it's not to see the sights, or to experience this place or that one. It's because they need to get away. They'll decide one day that they need to go to someplace like Disneyland: someplace fun, someplace that doesn't feel like it belongs in this world, the opposite of what they know. This is not a simple decision. They'll take weeks to research the costs, how far they'll have to travel, when it might fit workably into their schedules. But finally, they'll take the plunge and go. Life is getting the best of them and their curiosity is piqued.

"They have a lot of fun for a while when they get there, and wonder why it is that they don't live in a place like this, or visit more often. They ride the rides and eat the food and buy the souvenirs. We went to Disneyland once, your mother and you and I. Do you remember?"

I said I didn't. I was three.

"Well, you loved it. We all did. There are classier places to go on vacation, I know. You can go to Paris, or Prague, or London. These are places with a rich cultural history, any sort of history, they're places where you can learn about much more than the place itself. At Disneyland, though, you can't learn about anything but Disneyland, but that doesn't matter because for the time that you're there, you don't want to learn anyway. You left your common sense at home. And this is probably why a month is too long, among other reasons. This is the point I want to get across to you. Eventually they all realize that this isn't life, that they have to get back to what passes for the real world, that you can't live in Disneyland. There's nothing permanent there, or nothing worth permanence. Do you understand what I'm saying here?"

I nodded. The party was in an hour and I still had to shower and put on the new dress I'd just bought. He nodded back but didn't hug me, as I thought he might—Dad wasn't a hugger but he wasn't a shoulder-patter, either, and this seemed like a time for him to act unlike the version of himself he'd been so strict to present to me my whole life. He got up and grabbed a Gatorade, one of the only items in the kitchen, from the fridge, downed it in one lift of the bottle to his lips, and walked upstairs to his room without a word. He stayed in there the rest of the night and I had to walk to the party.

I didn't think much about what he'd told me (my asking him was what kissing me had been to Penny: just a lark, really) and had fun with my friends that night. I got a girlfriend only a month later, whom my mom liked but who never met my father, broke up with her just before college, dated several more women and lived with one. Almost all of these women except Beth lasted for only a month, and yet curiously I never thought of my father's advice after any of them. I haven't thought of it at all, in fact, until this morning, just after Beth moved her stuff out. What I thought about wasn't so much what he'd told me, but instead what my mom said to me when I got home from the party later that night.

Dad says he's like Disneyland, I told her, and when she rolled her eyes and asked why, I told her the gist of what he'd said. She responded by telling me that he didn't know his ass from a hole in the ground, but more importantly she told me that it was true, in a sense, that my dad was like Disneyland. He complains about women only loving Disneyland for a short time, she said, when the real problem is that Disneyland doesn't love anybody back, by which I think she meant that Disneyland loves everyone equally.

———

3. Home Sweet Home

Home Sweet Home.

So my plane gets in early and there's zero to do in my home town—which I haven't visited in three years—but I remember that if there's a place to be on a Saturday night in Midland Park, New Jersey, it's Legends. You know, Legends. Every town has one. Not Legends specifically but a townie bar of its ilk: shittily lit, oak tables, dance floor dimpled and pock-marked like it's got acne. I take a look around the place and I recognize not a soul, which, to give you context, when I was coming here nightly for those few years after high school when I didn't have my shit together and I was living in my mom's attic—during those years we knew everyone at Legends, this place was like our living room, actually I probably knew more people at Legends than at my own house considering how seldom I knew the names of the guys my mom brought home. But since then the crowd I used to go with has gotten older, traded in their Irish car bombs and beer bottles for German car dealers and baby bottles. Anyway I don't know anyone here right now and I'm about to 180 and put a Ted-shaped hole in the north wall when I see Horse at the end of the bar, watching the game. Horse: former Midland Park High School quarterback. Horse: who had more sex our freshman year of high school than I've had my entire life. Horse: who's right now sitting alone, slumped in his chair, waving me over like he's been expecting me.

What have you been up to Horse I ask, and he smiles like it's all one big joke, and it is, life, for him. *Getting thrown out of ex-girlfriends'* houses he says. *Getting thrown out of bars. You know how it is.* I don't, but I half-smile anyway, making sure not to fully smile since it's difficult to forget when Horse was twelve and it wasn't girlfriends or bouncers turning him away but his own father. It's easy to surmise that Horse's life has been basically a series of getting kicked out of places where he thought he felt home sweet home.

It's a small shitty bar in a small shitty town where everyone knows everyone else's shit, and I wonder momentarily if Horse knows what I've been up to, and it's like he can read my mind because he says *How's it out there? ASU right?* and I say *U of A* to the TV screen where, sure enough, the Wildcats are showing the Sun Devils what's what up and down the field as we speak. The cameras pan to a shot of the cheerleaders and Horse says *The chicks must be smoking hot at that school, huh?* And I say *Well they're my students,* in a tone where I may as well be saying they're my daughters, *So it's not really like that.* He raises his hand at the bartender like a man hailing a cab. *Smokin hot* he says, and flicks my sternum to punctuate each word. I insist that he not pay for my beer, I mean I'm not exactly planning on staying here with him if you get me, but there must be some secret Jerseyan handshake I've forgotten because the bartender's already popping the tops off our beers before I can say anything, so I say *You smoke* and he goes *Cigarettes?* and I nod, and he's already grabbing his coat with one hand and patting the small of my back with that quarterback's mix of fuck-you and good-to-see-ya as we walk out.

Real quick so this one thing about Horse: our senior year of high school I threw a party when my dad went away for the weekend, and Lindsay Allen broke up with me at it—at my own fucking party at my own fucking house she did it, I swear to God—and so I figured fuck it, it's my party and I'll cry if I want to, so I just went upstairs to mope in my bedroom until the last person left and I had to clean up. But when I got up there I saw Horse dangling one of my dad's cats upside down by his tail and the other cat under the bed and I went *What the hell are you doing,* me, I said that, all 90 pounds of me at the time, to Horse, the school quarterback, who even at seventeen looked like a well-built full-grown man; Horse, who two nights later had sex with Lindsay himself. But at that second I was drunk and all I saw was someone fucking with my dad's cats on the night the first girl I ever loved broke my heart. So I said *Get the hell out of here* and he put the cat down and shrugged and walked past me—no pun intended—with his tail between his legs and I checked to see if the cats were okay, and before I knew it Horse had my throat in his grip, my head against the wall, his face turning purple like he was the one being choked, talking through those huge two front teeth that earned him his nickname, saying *Don't ever. Fucking. Talk to me like that. Again.*

I'm telling you this because it's what I'm thinking about right now while we're outside smoking my cigarettes together, the professor and the quarterback—I wonder if he remembers nearly choking me to death, but I can't bring it up because I'm looking at him now and he doesn't look like the quarterback, I know it's a cliché but this is a true story, what am I supposed to say, Horse really looks like this: beer gut, barely any hair left, baggy eyes. I couldn't feel any worse for him if he himself was a cat being tortured by a sadistic seventeen-year-old. So instead I just say *What are you doing for work, Horse?* And he goes *Pipes, underground piping, wall piping, that kind of thing* and I open my mouth to respond despite the lack of anything on my tongue's tip since I'd be hard pressed to name a corner of the world I know less about, but he lets me off the hook when he says *I'm basically a glorified plumber, not anything as fun as ASU I'm sure* and I go *U of A* and he just keeps it up while he stares at the window advertising 99 cent hot dogs at 7-11, he says *I was gonna go to Australia, there's this program at work where they send you for five months and you learn more about piping and water systems down there*, at which comment I can't help myself and so say *I'm sure it's eye-opening to work with toilet water that spins clockwise*, which joke he either doesn't appreciate or doesn't get because he just goes *I dunno* and stares at the two blonde teenagers walking out of 7-11 with red bulls in hand, I mean they're seventeen years old if they're a day and Horse is staring at them hungrily, like they themselves are 99 cent hot dogs, and they're pretending not to notice in that teenagery way where let's face it they clearly do notice and I'm feeling really uncomfortable until Horse goes, *Hey, I wanna show you something.*

One more thing about Horse before I get to this last part. I haven't seen him in probably eightish years and sure part of that is because I moved out to Arizona five years ago but more generally it's because of the fundamentally divergent paths our lives have taken since we graduated high school a decade ago. Horse went to Springfield University on a full football scholarship for exactly one semester until—and again I know this is a cliché but again I don't know how to avoid cliché when you're doing nothing more than recapping the facts of someone's life—Horse got kicked out for drinking too much one night and wrapping his car around a lamppost in the parking lot of the student union. Kicked out, mind you, from yet another place he was supposed to feel home sweet home. After that I saw him a fair amount, this was when I was still going to Legends and Horse's face started appearing more and more right around the time mine was appearing less and less, and he basically just lived at home with his mom and drank until one night he got arrested for having sex with a fifteen-year-old and went to prison for three years—he'd wanted to become a gym teacher but obviously those three years more or less eviscerated that plan, hence I guess the plumbing—and when he got released he moved back in with his mom, who died of breast cancer this past January and left her house to him.

We're standing in said house right now, in its carpeted living room with its floral wallpaper, the lights are off and we're looking at the fireplace which is surrounded by kind of basically what you'd call a shrine if not a full on memorial, actually you're all from Tucson so here you go: what it looks like is the sign outside Gabby Giffords' office c. February 2011 when the whole community came together and decorated the place with flowers and banners of support, except instead of flowers this whole thing is covered in pictures of Horse's mom. There might be a hundred and it's her at every age, she has short hair and dark hair and long hair and light hair and 80s hair and 90s hair and in nearly all of them Horse is with her, and in nearly all of those she's holding him somehow, in her arms when he's a newborn and on her shoulders after a little league game and in an embrace at our graduation, and in all of these pictures Horse looks like—well, he looks home sweet home. She was pretty, Horse's mom, and we used to give him shit for that, as you do, and I feel like an asshole right now because all I can think of is Gene Hackman's line from *The Royal Tenenbaums: I'm sorry for your loss, your mother was a terribly attractive woman.* Instead thank god I just say *What is that,* meaning the shrine, even though I know the actual proper word for it. *That's my mom* he says, and his tone is weird, like I'm a stranger he's introducing to her, like we're looking right now at the woman herself. I try not to flinch. I still haven't stopped in to my own mother's yet, and I can't figure out why. *She liked this thing,* he says, this thing he doesn't know the word for, so I figured I'd make it nice for her. It looks like he's gonna cry any second, not sob or wail but something quieter, like someone trying to stifle a yawn, and he says *She missed me a lot when I was away,* and we let the words "in prison" float around for someone to catch but no one does. I think of Tucson and want to cheer him up so say *They have this thing called the Day of the Dead parade in Tucson. Where we celebrate the lives of people who've recently died.* He just keeps looking at what he's made so I go on. *That I point at it is called a "retable." It's a French word but I think it originated in Latin. It's an unattractive word but I almost like that. There's a kind of music in its clumsiness. In what it means.* He looks at me like he's just been slapped. *Ted,* he spits my name like a curse, *that's always been your problem. You can never just call something what it is,* and he turns back to the pictures and says *That's my mom,* and then says it a few more times, as though the repetition will help everything make sense: *That's my mom, that's my mom.*

———

4. Host

Host.

A prospective student visits, to find out whether he wants to attend our program. I don't meet him. He's only gone three weeks when Jax calls me and tells me she thinks she might have hepatitis C.

"I'm going to the doctor tomorrow. Can you drive me?" she asks. It's the first time we've spoken since we broke up in January. This is March.

"Drive you?" I say. "You're the one who has a car."

"I guess I just meant…can you go with me? My mind is a mess. I won't be able to concentrate on anything."

"Can't you just ask Jen or somebody?"

"If you're busy, I understand," she says.

But I'm not, of course. It's spring break, so I don't have to teach, and all I've done since Friday when classes let out is drink wine and walk Honey. I look at the empty bottles on top of the fridge, lined up like trophies in a case. I take out a pen to write on my arm. "What time is the appointment?"

.   .   .

Campus Health Services makes us sit in the lobby filling out paperwork before the actual check-up happens. Jax sits next to me with a clipboard in hand, writing and then sucking the end of the pen and then scratching out what she wrote, like someone taking an algebra test. It's true that she looks worn down, and I recognize how stressed she really must be: her eyes are sunken in from lack of sleep, her lips are so chapped they're cracking, her knobby wrists look almost broken. She must have lost ten pounds since I last saw her, nearly a tenth of her weight.

"This place smells like static," I say. "All doctors' offices do."

She doesn't stop writing, doesn't look up, but says, "Static doesn't have a smell," and I say, "Sure it does," and she says, "What does it smell like?" and I say, "This place," and she keeps on writing.

The other people waiting are invariably and fervently undergraduate: Wildcats hoodies with matching sweatpants, eyes glued to their iPhones, Adidas sandals with Wigwam socks. This is routine for them; they drink and they fuck and they make mistakes, and when they sober up they come here, and I think *We're here too* and I think *Jesus Christ* and I think *This is the culture that Jax and I live in.*

I look at her and can't help myself. "So did he stay with you while he was here?"

That stops her. She meets my eyes. I read the pink calligraphy of hers. "Is this really a conversation you want to have here?" she asks.

"I'm just asking. Just curious."

"He crashed at a bunch of people's places. He crashed at Kirk's house one night."

"But you put him up too? He was in the house?" Her knuckles turn white.

"Sorry," I say. "I'll stop."

She keeps writing and I lean over to her, "That head nurse is a dead ringer for Gene Hackman, don't you think?" and the sentence is barely out before she says, "You don't have to make me laugh," though for the first time all day I do hear something related to laughter, laughter's second cousin, in her voice, "I just need you to be here. To just sit there," she says and I say, "If that's what you need me to do," and she says, "That's what I need you to do." So we sit as she fills the rest of the thing out and the nurse calls *Ashley?* and the nurse calls *Nikki?* and the nurse calls *Holly?* and *Amber?* and *Tiffani?* and finally Jax hands me the clipboard. "Can you look it over before we go in? My brain's so scrambled, I feel like I forgot my own birthday."

But before I get a chance to, the nurse calls Jax's name, and she looks at me while the nurse looks at her, squints *Are you going to come in* and I raise my eyebrows and nod *Do you want me to come in* and she winces and raises her chin *If you're comfortable with that* and we're good at conversations like this, eye dialogue.

.   .   .

In the office I stand there like an idiot and the doctor, a lady doctor, seems to have no idea what I'm doing in here. I don't say anything to clarify the situation. Neither does Jax.

"Any drugs?" the doctor asks and Jax says no, no drugs which is no surprise to me and the doctor says "Drinking?" and she says no, which I also know she doesn't do but am actually surprised by the answer for some reason, maybe because I can't imagine a life without booze anymore, and the doctor says "Are you sexually active?" and Jax pauses and I do my absolute best not to flinch when she says "Yes", and then the nurse turns to *me* and asks whether *I'm* sexually active, I guess because she assumes Jax and I are together, and I go, "Me? No, I'm sexually passive," but neither of them laugh.

I try to tune the interrogation out by thinking about what I have to do the rest of the day, which is write a little and drink a little and pick up food for Honey. We found the dog together, me and Jax, last fall when things were good or goodish, and now Honey lives with me, a permanent guest in my house, this twenty-four hour a day remnant of Jax that I have to feed and nurture and keep alive.

.   .   .

I'm not allowed in the lab where they have to take her blood and stuff, which ironically is the one place she actually needs me to be. So I go outside to smoke a cigarette as I let her answers sink in, the implications, the sleep I'm going to lose, until I feel a tap on my shoulder and turn to see Moriah, one of my students.

"Hey," she says. "Got a light?"

Moriah's a good student. Doesn't talk a lot in class—not because she's shy, but because she thinks she's a lot smarter than all the other students. Which she is, but I don't tell her that.

I hold my lighter to her cigarette. "What are you doing here?"

Her eyes bulge as she puffs, caught off guard or mock-caught off guard by the question. "Same thing as you, I guess," she says and nods at the sign that says "Women's Health."

There's no way I'm not blushing. "I meant why aren't you home for spring break?"

"I am," she says. "I'm from Tucson."

"Right," I say, though I don't think I ever knew that.

We smoke for a few minutes in silence until she says, "What are you in for?"

"Are you supposed to ask me that?"

"Dunno. You don't have to answer."

But I haven't talked to anyone who isn't my dog for weeks, and so I do. "It's not me. I'm here with a friend."

"A *lady* friend?"

I roll my eyes at her and blow out my response with the smoke. "Why are you here?"

"Are you supposed to ask *me* that?"

I shrug.

"My idiot boyfriend."

"Uh oh. What'd he do?"

"No—it's not like that. He's just really careful. Wants me to get tested before we...you know."

"Responsible."

"You think?"

"You guys are how old?"

"Twenty."

I try to think of what I was like at that age but come up short. Did I love my girlfriend at the time? Who was I even dating at twenty?

She must feel awkward standing there as I think, because she says, "We've been together since the end of high school. You have no *idea* what a butthead he can be."

"So why're you with him?"

"I'm an even bigger butthead." By which I don't think she means: I don't know what I'm doing. I think she means: We love each other in spite of this stuff.

"Don't worry," I say. "You're still young."

"What changes?" she asks.

I put out my cigarette. Then I look at her and shrug.

.　　　.　　　.

When the test is done Jax buys me lunch to say thank you and then we walk Violet and Honey in the park together and don't say much.

"How's she doing?" asks Jax, nodding at Honey.

"Good. We're getting used to each other."

The dogs are kicking up dirt and sniffing whatever's underneath. Jax looks around the park and says, "This is the first place we ever hung out alone."

I think back to those weeks after she first moved to town, when I first met her and put on the full court press to get her to hang out with me. She'd been with someone at the time.

"Going for a walk with the dog was the only surefire way I could think of to get you alone," I say and she says, "That was smart," and I go, "I have my moments." She smiles and says, "You cut poop off Violet's butt for me that day," and I go, "Oh yeah," almost in spite of myself, "with the sewing scissors. From your bag," and she says, "That's the most romantic thing anyone's ever done for me."

One week from now, she gets her test results back. They're negative. But she keeps stressing anyway, convinced the virus is just dormant and hasn't shown up yet.

One month from now, she writes an essay about the process of waiting for the results and the anxiety it provokes. In it, she lists celebrities who've contracted hepatitis C—Pamela Anderson, Kid Rock. She spells Allen Ginsberg's name wrong three different ways. I'm not mentioned in it.

One year from now, the essay gets published in a pretty high-profile journal. By that time, we're dating again after three more break-ups, so I buy her dinner to celebrate.

But that's all in the future. Right now, we lie down on the grass next to each other, as unsure of what the other's thinking as we've ever been. I reach my hand out for hers and she holds it back. It's the first time we've touched each other in weeks.

"Thanks for coming today, Theo," she says.

I shrug. I don't remember when I became such an adamant shrugger.

"This doesn't mean we're talking again," I tell her.

"I know," she says.

———

5. Anhedonia.

Anhedonia.

So we're on our way to the restaurant when the kid turns to me and she goes, *Dad, who is this lady?* Just like that she says it, *Who is this lady*, eight years old and already she sounds like a snotty teenager, which she just so clearly gets from her mother that it isn't even worth going into. *She's a friend* I say, and keep my eyes on the traffic, *I already told you who she is*, because I did, like six times back at the house. But there's something about my explanation she doesn't like or trust. *Is this a date?* she asks. *No* I say, too quick, less because I'm lying than because I'm surprised she knows yet what a date is, until I realize that of course fucking Janine fucking told her, which realization is confirmed when she says, *Because I don't think Mom would like you taking me on a date* and then a Range Rover of all goddam things cuts me off. *Well then*, I tell her, *your mother should call me before she drops you off out of the blue, kiddo. I mean don't get me wrong, I love having you here, but I didn't exactly know you'd be around tonight.* Danielle shrugs, *She had an emergency*, and stares at her own reflection in the side-view mirror as I change lanes. I'm wondering what she sees there—if she sees what I see whenever I look at her little face: my puggish nose, my widow's peak—but everything else is Janine's, especially like now, like when she's pouting and lippy and feeling sorry for herself. I feel like such a shit for even thinking that, though, that I try to make it up to her and say *Get whatever you want tonight. Chicken fingers, right?* That wins her from the mirror, though she doesn't smile. She's still being mad at me. *With honey mustard?* she asks. There's a lilt in her voice despite her effort to punish me. *Who is this lady* she says once more under her breath, and though I shouldn't react, I go *It's not a date* again because fuck it, if she's already turning into her mother, I might as well start lying to her.

We're (I'm) not supposed to meet Amanda until 7:30 and we're in the parking lot of Chili's by quarter after so we idle in a space wordlessly, and really even though I don't want Dani and Amanda in the same restaurant in the same room at the same *table*, for God's sake—but then whatareyougonnado, it's Friday and it's happy hour and it's not like I'm taking the kid to a dive bar right, I mean what am I gonna leave her at home by herself with a Pixar movie? blow Amanda off and babysit?—I find myself tapping the brake pedal in anticipation with tremors that can only be described as Parkinsonian. I'm smoking my way through half a pack of Camels and Dani is playing with the radio until she finds a country station, some singer whose voice I recognize but can't name. *Okay your turn* I say, this little game of ours, *what's this one babe?* She looks at the dome light and goes *Yodeling. Yodeling and* but she stops so I go *Yodeling and what,* and she goes *Yodeling and sand,* sand, I'm guessing, because the singer's got a gravelly voice, so I nod and she twiddles the knobs again and I look at the Chili's entrance for Amanda and try to remember what she looks like, try to guess what she'll wear. Last night when we met she was wearing cut-off Daisy Dukes and a not really like a tank top but more like what looked like an oversized handkerchief tied around her torso, right here she was wearing it, at this very Chili's, and of course none of the meathead-y bartenders seemed to mind. She was drinking something called an El Presidente straight out of a plastic mixer with the words "MARGARITA MADNESS" on the side, a drink whose salt I could smell on her breath when she leaned in and said *You look like* before being interrupted by the bouncer, or whatever the equivalent of a bouncer is at Chili's, who told her she probably needed to head out, and I promised I'd get her home safe and we Frenched in my car before I took her back to my place where the sex was fine, but really didn't compare to the thought I had back in the car, which was that it had been so long since I'd Frenched someone that I didn't even know what the cool word for Frenching was anymore. I have absolutely no idea what Dani will think of someone like Amanda and I don't know what she'll tell Janine and so as you can see the Parkinsonian leg tremors are a bit understandable considering the balancing act I'm about to pull off, but I can't think of any of that anyway because Dani goes *Dad-dy, your turn!* to a radio station that sounds like the Cranberries, a B-side, from *Everybody Else is Doing it, So Why Can't We* I think, and if I want to play the game properly, I have to answer honestly, but the only answer on the tip of my tongue—which I don't dare say to Dani—is *Your mom, this one sounds like your mom,* and it does, though it sounds like the old Janine. The new Janine sounds like, well, she sounds like Dani, right now, as in this second in the parking lot, as Dani looks toward the entrance and says, *Oh, I'll just bet that's her.*

Right right context: okay. What do you want to know? Would it help to know that Janine and I broke up a year ago? Would it help to know neither of us can afford a lawyer, hence we're not technically legally divorced, hence no custody agreement, hence Dani being dropped in my lap whenever Janine doesn't feel like being a parent for a night? Would it help to know that I've tried to get back together like nine times? Or that I'm not in the least bit paranoid when I say that my daughter is being turned against me? Or that it's working? Or that I sound so much like my father when I say that that I have to sit on my balcony and chain smoke until the taste of him disappears? Probably not. Probably all you really need to know is this: Janine is convinced both that I'm an alcoholic and that I don't love her anymore, but she's only right about one.

This is where Amanda comes in. She's sitting between Dani and me, and she's already handled my bringing an eight year old on our date with really you gotta hand it to her and just call it aplomb, like this was the plan the whole time, like *of course* I was gonna bring my daughter along, why would she think otherwise, what's happy hour without a first-grader in tow? Dani is looking around the bar at the crowd that's here, mostly young pant-suited chicks and a couple guys in shirtsleeves who just got off their telemarketing jobs and are trying to forget the nine to five for a night. The crowd to our left cracks up at something, way too loud, and Dani giggles too. *What are you laughing at* asks Amanda, genuine though, not mean, just sweet and curious, and Dani picks up on it and goes *It's so funny, they're so funny, why are they acting so funny* and we look over at the group where one of the guys has poured the margarita salt on the table and is pretending to snort it like coke. *They're happy* Amanda says. *What are they happy about* Dani asks, and I go *Beer, babe. They're happy about beer.* Amanda puts her hand on my knee under the table and I arch my neck around for the waiter before she can catch my eye, but she puts a finger to my chin and turns my head to hers anyway. *Hey you* she says, and as the words reach my nose there's a tar-and-citrus sting that I do my best not to flinch at. *You know what you want* I ask her and Dani goes *Chicken fingers I thought*, until she looks up from her menu and sees this woman wrapped around her father like a strait jacket and realizes I wasn't talking to her. But Amanda turns and says *Chicken fingers sounds great. I haven't had those in forever, you wanna share some* but Dani obviously doesn't and looks almost personally offended that anyone would want to share hers, and then Amanda goes *I like them with honey mustard, you?* and Dani smiles and for a second I think, *Shit, maybe this will work.*

So I get a drink and Amanda gets a drink and for Dani we order Pepsi, chicken fingers, mozzarella sticks, whatever she wants—just as long as she stays entertained. *Eat some* I tell Amanda, pointing to the appetizer plate, *it'll soak up whatever's in that glass.* She slides her hand up my thigh another inch and swivels her head to Dani, says *Is your dad always this much of a square?* Dani, mouth full of scalding hot cheese, goes *Square,* her mouth too full for me to tell if it's a question or what, so Amanda just makes a little square with her pointer fingers and says *I'm gonna use the bathroom* and uses my crotch as a platform to lift herself up.

She's all right huh I say to Dani as soon as Amanda gets up, and Dani just shrugs, not even looking at me when she does it either, looking instead at the chicken finger in her hand that she tears into pieces until it's the shape of a gun. *Bang* she says, pointing her chicken-gun at me and I go *Where'd you pick that up*, meaning the habit obviously, not the chicken finger, and she says *This boy in class*—you hear that? A boy from class. First grade! Or at least I think that's what grade she's in—*Robby* she continues as I gain my composure enough to hear her out, *I hate him, he keeps following me and bugging me every time I try to talk to people.* I watch her dip the barrel of the gun into some honey mustard and say *He probably just likes you, you're pretty* which she is kind of, for an eight year old anyway, and she says *I don't want him to like me. I hate him.* I order another whiskey Coke (I like hearing about how her life is going and I want to enjoy it) in anticipation of her follow up, I want to hear why she hates him, what this poor kid did to deserve her hatred, to make her not want him around her when clearly that's all he wants, but it takes her until the drink arrives to say *Where'd you meet Amanda?*

Here I say, walking through the fucking minefield of this conversation, careful only to say where we met and not when, and wondering where the hell Amanda is anyway. *Did you and Mom meet at a bar* she asks and I say *This isn't a date* and she says *Did you though* and I say *This isn't like me and Mom* and she says *But did you* and I say *No, your mother and I met in college.* Something just absolutely fantastic must have just happened in the Yankees game because the margarita-coke-salt guys at the bar explode at the screen in fireworks of laughter so I can't hear what my daughter says next and I say *What? What hun?* and she says *How I said*, and I have to think a minute to remember. *When you're in college it's like camp* I tell her, *You all live together, boys and girls, and Mom lived across the hall from me. I was really scrawny* and she says *What's scrawny* so I absentmindedly pat my own biceps, *It's when you're grown up but you still look like a little kid, real skinny,* and she says *You're still scrawny* but she says it "scron-ny", sounding out this new word she just learned, so I don't take offense. *Your mom was really pretty and for some reason she actually talked to me, like a lot, and so we got together and had you and that's when we had to leave school,* I say, surprised, actually, that Janine's never told her this story. *But* Dani says *how did you meet? That's how you knew each other but how did you meet?* which I'm confused at and say *You mean become boyfriend and girlfriend* and she goes *Yeah* and I say *Well*

Hope you two didn't miss me too much Amanda says, standing over us, clear-eyed and peppy and tall; I take her in for the first time and she's quite a sight, in this Greek-style dress that just fits her like a dream, I mean she's wearing the hell out of the thing and even Dani's gotta notice. *Of course we did* I say, *where were you?* She shakes her half-empty pack of Newports in response. She sits back down and says to Dani *They have a jukebox here. What music do you like,* and Dani says *I don't know. Dad has this one CD he lets me play on Saturdays when I'm over there. It's called Golden Oldies. I like those guys.* And here Amanda's face lights up *bam!* like Dani has just said the magic words. *Fifties stuff?* Amanda asks her and Dani goes *Maybe* and I say *Yes* and Amanda says *Dion and the Belmonts?* which lands on Dani's ears like Shakespeare in Greek as translated by Siamese cats, so Amanda starts to sing *Here's a story, it's sad but true/ About a girl that I once knew...* And if you knew my daughter you'd understand that this is all it takes: Dani belts out the rest of "Runaround Sue", note-perfect, and Amanda doesn't try to out-sing her, just accompanies her with some *hey-hey-bumpahaydeehaydee-hey-hey, awwwwwww's*—in other words she's the Belmonts, not Dion—and Amanda even does a little Chaplinesque tap dance with the chicken fingers and I'm wondering where all this energy is coming from, but don't bother myself with it, just order another round for all three of us.

I lean back and relax a second, the food's gone but the drinks are still coming and I think I can leave these two alone for a beat, though Amanda won't sit still and even Dani is wiggling all around. I'm about to say *What's the matter sweetie* but Amanda says *What's the matter sweetie* and Dani says *My shirt, my shirt itches, it's the tag,* and Amanda takes a pair of tiny scissors from her purse and helps to cut it off as she says *Have you ever heard of a hair shirt?* which Jesus Christ of course my daughter hasn't, but those two seemingly disconnected nouns sound funny to an eight year old when put together so Dani's interest is piqued. *Take it easy* I tell Amanda and she just brushes it off. *It's a really uncomfortable shirt people used to wear. They made it out of horse hair.*

Gross! Dani says, in that way little kids say "gross!", the way adults normally say "delicious!" *Why would they wear something like that? It sounds itchy.*

It was, says Amanda. *That was the point. They did it when they felt bad about stuff. To show they were sorry* she says and sips her drink and I sip mine. I'm actually kind of impressed with the way Amanda's explained this without any kind of religious context whatsoever, and I'm feeling a little buzz from the bubbles crawling down my throat so I let her keep going. *When I was a kid, my dad didn't talk to me all that much, he knew I loved baseball but he didn't know what team. He thought I liked the Red Sox even though I loved the Yankees* which is funny since she hasn't turned her head to the screen once this whole time, but whatever, *so for my birthday one year he bought me this Red Sox hat and I hated it. But I never threw it out. Every time I messed up or did something he didn't like, if I got a bad grade or skipped school or got kicked out for fooling around with a boy in the janitor's closet, I'd wear it for him, in front of him, so he'd know* she says, and I don't know if Dani knows what "fooling around" is but maybe you just have to be here, at this table, watching Amanda tell this story—she's so kidlike and manic and invested in telling it that interrupting her just feels cruel, and I'm about to put a hand on her shoulder, seriously that's how wounded she seems at the sound of this memory, but before I can get my hand there she shoots up out her chair and says *I have to pee again* and I notice for the first time her sniffling and rubbing her nose as she picks up her purse and walks away.

Dani on the other hand doesn't seem to have noticed at all, she's a pretty perceptive kid but maybe that only applies when it comes to me and her mom. She knew this was a date, for instance, and she knows whenever Janine has guys over that they aren't just pals, I know Dani can see right through it because she tells me, whenever I ask. I ask Dani about Janine's personal life a lot, and if you think that's pathetic and manipulative you're not telling me anything I don't already know. But before you judge me, although I'm sure you've already done so, just try to imagine someone you've loved, an ex, someone whose rejection of you is a total mystery, and now imagine that you have a little person living with that ex who carries around this well of information, and now imagine this little person hanging around your house for days at a time unexpectedly, and now try to resist the temptation to ask and ask and ask and ask. Dani is my daughter but she's also like my personal human wiretap, even if asking her about Janine's dating life is like a sort-of emotional hair shirt in itself.

Fuck I hear, loud and clear as someone calling my name for dinner, and here's the part I want to tell you about. Those assholes at the bar have gone from hitting on the girls next to them to straight-up harassment. A blonde guy with a buzz cut and a loosened, slack tie reaches for one girl's purse. *Hey* she says *give that back* and he goes *Not until you guys promise to come down the street with us*, and her friend says *Quit being an asshole* and I'm happy that at least the two girls are in it together until I realize that Girl #2 is not talking to Buzz Cut but is in fact talking to Girl #1, telling her not to be an asshole by, I don't know, *allowing* this dickhead to steal her purse, and the swearing is getting super loud so I check Dani's face—unfazed thank God since we are after all at a bar and I can't after all make them stop swearing, but I certainly *can* say something to Buzz Cut, I've got liquor muscles now and want to show my daughter what her dad is made of, I want to give her something to report back to Janine that isn't just Dad-introduced-me-to-his-friend-at-the-bar, or hey-Mom-do-you-know-what-a-hair-shirt-is, or have-you-ever-heard-of-an-El-Presidente, I want Janine to know I am not a guy but a *man*. I want to be the old me in the same way that for years now I've been wanting Janine to be the old Janine, and so I get up and grab this girl's purse, just like that I grab it, sans resistance, and Buzz Cut looks not at me but at the girl, looks at her like she just broke his heart, like she just returned his engagement ring or turned him down for the prom or something. I'm starting to think I've misread the situation and begin to say *Hey I'm, I'm* and then I don't know what it is that comes over me but you have to just trust me on this, this is a true story so believe me, I was there, you weren't: I look at my daughter and she's still my daughter but she's twenty years old. Her hair's longer and her eyes are bigger and she's starting to get these little parenthetical lines at the corners of her mouth, but it's definitely her. And the look she gives me is so piercing that it's like she's not even looking at me, like I'm not even in front of her, like I don't even fucking *exist*, I'm tissue paper, I'm air, I'm nothing, and looking back at her I see her widow's peak is gone and she's grown in to her nose, so there's nothing left of me even in her—blame this all on the liquor if you like—but as soon as I blink she's back, Dani, Danielle, my girl, eight years old if she's a day, and it's at this point that I know something's supposed to occur to me, something about how to take care of her, some fatherly instinct is gonna kick in about the Amanda situation or about Buzz Cut or just about being there for my kid in general—but nothing does. Instead I just stand there with the purse still in my hand and I stare at my daughter and I think:

The morning before Janine realized she was pregnant with Dani, we were lying in my dorm room bed, a tiny single that barely fit me, let alone us. Finals were approaching, and Janine was going home to Minnesota for the whole summer, so we had no clue whether we'd stay together or even see each other again, since we were moving to different buildings next year. I didn't know whether she was awake yet, and when I opened my eyes all I wanted was a lumberjack breakfast—Janine could go hours without eating but I always woke up next to her hungry as a bear. Janine got out of bed and stretched and when she got to the window she said *Clouds*. I just looked at her against the window and saw her skinny little silhouette, gawky-sweet and maybe a little awkward, hair framing her face like a curtain. There was a bleach stain on her turquoise underwear. She asked if she could bum a cigarette so I gave her one, one of the last two in the pack. I'd been planning on quitting. I pulled on my pants. Outside, I saw the clouds rolling in.

She took out the cigarette I'd given her. She stood on the steps of the dorms and waited for me to light it so I lit it with the cherry of my own, leaned in to hers so the ends could kiss. She didn't step back but instead leaned in too. I smiled at her, which smile she tried to avoid, but I kept grinning at her like an idiot. She smiled back.
What, she said.

———

6. How to Start Again in Twelve Easy Steps

How to Start Again in Twelve Easy Steps.

(1) First and foremost: remember that you are a small man, a petty, petty man. Recall and appreciate the times—seldom though they may be—that you've been big. Cherish these, but keep in mind that, on the whole, you are a small and petty person. Don't attempt to decipher why you're like this. Make no attempt at locating the source of your small, petty nature. Accept it.

(2) When she calls, be happy. Relish the sound of the ringtone. Relish the sight of the blinking red light. Feel the relief, like the release of a sneeze, of these calls after months of silence. Keep this relief to yourself. Act casual as you answer. Choose your words carefully. Say "hey," and elongate the word to two syllables. Do not follow it with "baby" or "babe" or "gorgeous" or any of the other names you've used with the women you've dated since the breakup.

(3) Listen as she speaks. Nod, even if she can't see you doing it over the phone, as she tells you about her day; listen as she tells you about her friends who are engaged or married, or getting green cards or nose jobs; hear the words "nose jobs" and recall to yourself how, right after your breakup, you made the singular vow No More Rich Girls. Get sidetracked as you try to remember why No More Rich Girls seemed so important, why it seemed like the very nugget and core of everything that went wrong with you two last time, why it didn't just get chalked up to a difference between her Burberry scarves and the holes in your sleeve cuffs or between your use of "killer" as an adjective and her use of "summer" as a verb; stumble upon the half-forgotten realization that it was less *material* and more a question of *sensibility*, she having led a life of safety and therapy and you having not ever had the time to dwell on every. single. thought. you had. because you were too busy at your after-school job helping your mother make rent. Most importantly, push these feelings down because after all, she's apparently come to her senses and is now not only with you but presently, this second, as in right now as you're thinking this, on the phone with you during her lunch break, which sounds like no big deal but is actually a huge deal because she only has a few precious minutes during the day, and she values her free time and frankly would rather spend it alone, collecting her thoughts and re-charging her batteries—as a matter of fact (please keep in mind) she's still kinda on the fence about being alone in general, not just

during her lunch break but during the remainder of her life, she's trying on this relationship again like a sweater that feels comfortable but has gone out of fashion, she's testing it out because she can't tell if she wants to end up with *anyone* (let alone you) or if she'd rather live a life of solitude, and if the latter then she's confused about whether that's okay, which confusion had *a lot* to do with your break up six months ago and *everything* to do with the earlier instruction not to call her "baby" or "babe" or "gorgeous" etc, and anyway, Important Tidbit: do not lose track of the conversation. Her story—about her linguistics class this morning, in which she learned about the human brain's ability to compartmentalize several languages in its first two years—is coming to an end soon, and it will be your turn to speak.

Side Note: You'll run into this problem often, so do not try to avoid it. Learn that it comes with the territory. Learn that this is what happens when you date someone you know well, someone with whom you have a long and complicated history. Do not expect that any conversation you'll ever have again will be unencumbered by second-guessing and bifurcated thought processes. Think, but do not say, that you'd rather live this complicated life with her than a life of ease with anyone else. Realize that this is why you love her.

Here's where it gets tricky: Love love love love—the steps are simple for that part. Refer here to step (1); remember that you are a small and petty man.

(4) Hear her say, "…which is weird because Eli speaks three languages, but when I told him, he didn't get it." Feel every inch of your skin tighten elastically around your bones at those two syllables, Eli. Look down and conceptualize this skin-tightening, your muscles ropy and tense and pulsing. *Feel your teeth*—this sounds difficult, and is difficult to describe, but rest assured, it will come to you. Feel your teeth. They'll sting. But level your voice when you say, "Eli?"

(5) Realize too late that you interrupted her thought to say *Eli?* but don't apologize now. It will upset the trajectory of the conversation. Note the pregnant pause that follows, and word it to yourself mentally *(this is a pregnant pause)*. Listen to her break the silence, "Yeah, Eli."

(6) Ask, "When did you talk to Eli?" and make no attempt to sound neutral; there is no way for that sentence to sound anything but small and petty.

(7) Hear—you will be able to, impossible though it may sound—her eyes roll as she says, "Why do you have such a problem with Eli?" Note that she didn't answer your question.

(8) Say—mumble—growl—half under your breath—that in fact you *don't* have a fucking problem with fucking Eli, and expect her follow-up remark, learned no doubt in rich-person therapy: "Then why do you swear every single time you bring him up? He's just a guy. I liked plenty of other guys after you. Why is this one person such an issue?"

(9) Tread lightly, here. DO NOT lose your temper. Know that this is not an unwinnable fight—in fact, this potentially could not be a fight at all, just a conversation, even a progressive, pragmatic conversation that mends wounds that have been festering for six months, if you choose your words carefully. She will hear you out if you offer good common sense.

(10) Take a moment to answer the question, because as presumptuous and psychobabbly and invalidating of your totally justifiable feelings as it may be, you likely have not ever articulated its answer to yourself.

Why do you have such a problem with Eli?

Possible answer #1: Absorb yourself in the memory of the previous June, when this Eli asshole visited town. Recall the morning that you were walking your dog—the dog you'd bought together, but was then your responsibility and now both of yours again—in your shitty sweatpants and *I just woke up* hair and torn t-shirt; recall how hung-over you were from another in a series of whiskey-stained nights getting over her; recall the two of them driving past the dog park and slowing down just for a second; recall this prick's face peering out from the passenger side window of her car, this prick in expensive-looking Oakleys and a muscle t-shirt (a fucking jock! what are we, in seventh grade? remember thinking); remember the honking of the horn and recall wondering about whatever stupid face you must have been making as the dog took a shit at that exact moment and this fucking asshole laughed and the car zoomed away, trailing echoes of asshole-laughter behind it where you stood. Conclude that this isn't the right answer—just a moment, a memory, a horrible embarrassment. Think again.

Possible answer #2: Visualize the pictures that popped up everywhere, all over the internet, from that weekend he visited. Try to get the title of her photo album right—something stupid, some inside joke between the two of them, a joke so inside that you wondered why she was posting it publicly in the first place, unless it was just to piss you off; then wonder if that's it, wonder if you're mad because they tried to piss you off together. But dismiss this answer because, frankly, she was so over you at that point (you know for a fact) that there's just no way you had that much to do with her motives. So,

Possible answer #3: Hear the ghosts of conversations from the first time you were together, posit that your reason for having such a problem with Eli is that you've been told not to have a problem with Eli before, you were told like a million times, in fact, were made to feel like a jealous irrational baby last time around for suspecting something might have been up with those two, were incensed at the fact that he booked his ticket to visit her like a week after you broke up, the body wasn't even cold yet!, and then he shows up and they go to the fucking Grand fucking Canyon together for one fucking weekend and suddenly she's in fucking love, note the frequency of your cursing here and suggest to yourself that maybe you've found the root this time, maybe answer #3 is just the ticket, the justification you could offer gladly and even calmly (so rational is this logic) but then conclude that this is a dead-end too because you know what she'll say (she's said it before, last June, when you totally overstepped your boundaries and forced her to talk to you about it), which is that love is a mystery and that feelings can develop where there were no feelings before, and feelings can die where once they were strong, and that we never know why we feel this way or when our feelings can crop up or stop dead, and so practical (if sad) is this truth that it will be impossible to refute—so don't try—and further it will point toward and unearth some other pretty touchy subjects, namely what it was that made you two break up in the first place, and what it is that's keeping you on such thin ice now: her total belief (see: fear) that if either of the two of you commit today then the other of the two of you will flake out tomorrow, her total belief (see: fear) that feelings are unsustainable and unpredictable and that there are limits to love.

And while you're at it, (11) ask yourself: who the fuck do you think you are? Whoever she saw when you weren't together is none of your business, really, so why don't you get over yourself and recognize that people deal with these things in their own ways and just because those ways are different from your own doesn't make them wrong, okay she isn't perfect but you sure as shit aren't either, and anyway it's not like you're some paragon of fidelity here, you haven't exactly been living the last six months like a monk, staring at her picture every day, okay that doesn't make her right but that doesn't make you right either because the point is that no one is "right" in these things, what you really are is just two scared, fragile, confused people who happen to be in love. Open your mouth to articulate all this to her but get cut off when she says, "This is really hard, isn't it?" Say, "Yeah, it is," and feel your stomach, by pure muscle memory, brace itself for the break up, until she says, gently, "We'll stay afloat." Feel weirdly unsurprised by this, because hey, it's true, and it's said with love, and hell, it can't be easy for her to be this big in reaction to you being so, so small, it can't be easy for her to actually not make you feel small at all, to throw herself under the bus just to make you feel okay, it can't be easy for her to do this every. single. time. you talk.

(12) So just temper yourself. Swallow it all down—it's small, and therefore easy to swallow. Say, "Thank you," but not "I'm sorry" even though you are sorry. Tell her that you'd better let her go, isn't it almost time for class? Visualize her glancing at the clock as she says, "Oh shoot, good point." Hear her say, "I'd better go, message me later." Say, "Okay." Hear her say, "See you later, T-e-d." Hear the love in her voice. Admire her ability to maintain that love. Feel awed by the warmth of her weird and wild heart. Stay afloat. Stay afloat.

———

7. Negotiation

Negotiation.

Your fingernails are dirty and your clothes are stained with paint but that does not mean you are unprepared to meet with her right now. She pulls up the seat across from you and takes a breath as she sits—not a sigh, a breath, small but noticeable if you're paying attention to that kind of thing, which you are. She puts her stuff down before saying anything, lays it out in a row between you two like a barricade: her purse, her travel mug, and a book. She's brought a fucking *book* with her, which pisses you off until you notice it's a big fat collection of essays by Joan Didion, the one you bought her for Christmas that first year. She says *Hi* and you say *Hi* and she says *So* and you say *So* and you know this tactic, declining-to-speak-first; the foreman at work used it on you last time you asked for a raise. It's a little like chicken and a little like chess and you're great at both of those, so you look around the coffee shop for something to concentrate on as you wait her out. A middle-aged guy sits alone at the table adjacent, staring into his coffee, and he looks up expectantly when the door to the place opens, but his face falls when he doesn't recognize whoever walks in. *How's your mom* she asks and you go *Fine. Chemo starts next month. How's your dad* and she goes *Good. Operation was yesterday. They think they got it all* and you go *Great* and she goes *So* and there you sit. *Talk to me* she says, and you chew the skin on your thumb and say *What about.* She says *I'm trying to be honest. I want this to work but I want to see how things are* by which you know she means *I want to see how you've changed, how much you've changed, whether you've changed* which you can't really fault her for, because that's why you're here too. *Be honest with me* she says *even if it's cutting, even if it's something I might not want to hear.*

.   .   .

Four years ago, you met. It was a weekday, so of course you were at AB&G with the guys, knocking off another shit day on the site, building of all things some new frat house for the rich-bitch kids at the U. You were in the middle of a joke, the one about the priest and the hobo, syllables away from the punch line, when she walked in with a couple friends. She looked alien mixing with the working crowd, and you wondered why, as a white-trash Jersey Rick Blaine might have said, of all the shitty blue-collar bars in all the world, an upper-crust girl like her had walked into yours. She looked *written*, was the phrase in your head. Like the kind of girl you see in movies and go, *No one looks that good in real life.* She looked like the kind of girl

45

your dad warned you about, the only piece of advice you ever got from him. And then what were the odds, she ordered a shot of whiskey, and when you heard her order you knew what Nick Carraway meant when he said Daisy's voice sounded full of money. When you finally snapped out of it the guys were looking at you on the edge of their seats and you realized you hadn't finished your joke. But instead of finishing you got up—who knows where these balls were coming from, this was exactly not the kind of thing you'd ever do—you beelined up to her, paid for her drink, and said *Well hello there stranger.*

.   .   .

You light a cigarette. You know she hates that but she wants you to be honest. *I don't think I was fair to you last time around* you begin. *I thought you were perfect* and she says *Now you know I'm not* and you say *Now I know you're not. You're selfish and callow and you think you're capricious when what you really are is spoiled. You give yourself license to do whatever the hell you want.* You expect her to look away but to her credit she maintains eye contact and you think maybe she means it when she says she wants you to be honest. *What if that hasn't changed* she asks and you say *It hasn't* and she says *So what's different* and you say *What's different is that I'm those things too, and at least I know it now.* She closes her eyes and nods, like *No shit Sherlock*, though she has the couth not to actually say that. Instead she says *There's a good chance I'm not ready for this yet* and you say *I'm not either* and she looks at you like *Well what's the point then*, to which you say *But who cares. I don't care and you wouldn't be here if you did, either.* You expect this logic to win her over—it's inarguable, isn't it?—until she shrugs at you, says *You're more selfish than I am. You're ignoring what I'm saying. I think you have a problem with women, you don't think their needs outweigh yours* and you say *I don't have a problem with women, I have a problem with you* and she lets it drop but you aren't ready to because how dare she, *My needs outweigh yours?* She reaches across the barrier of purse-mug-book for your hand and goes *You can be exhausting. Be clear with me. That's why I'm here. What is it you want?*

.   .   .

Three years ago, you proposed. Not on your knee, not with a ring, not even consciously if you're honest. Just out of the blue. But in a way that kind of made it almost more sincere than if you'd planned it out. Here's how it happened: you'd both been drinking and she'd had a few more than you, which was the only time you could ever remember that happening. She'd spent so many nights taking care of you after your benders—placing cold washcloths to your head, or bringing you take-out to soak up the night— that it was nice to take care of her for once. You told her this as she nodded off: *It's nice to take care of you.* Maybe she was drunk, or maybe her guard was up, because she just said *Huh* and you said *You okay* and she said I *love you too*, which was the first time either of you had said that. You said *We should get married*, and really it was just a way to one-up her, but after it came out it sounded right, in a way the words you say to people never sound right, and she said (eyes closed) *That would be nice*, and it felt official, even though—with her in that state—the gesture felt cowardly, like shouting threats to people from your passing car, and you knew she'd wake up the next day with no memory of the night before, just regret and a cramp and a headache so blinding she swore she'd never do it again.

.   .   .

I want you say as you put out your cigarette *I want to be who I am with you all the time.* And she says *I want you to be able to be that whether I'm around or not*, and you say *I'm fine without you, really I am, I'm just better when I'm with you*, and she says *I need you to understand that I'm a lot of things and that only one of them is your ex-girlfriend, and that's far from the most important.* You nod and say *I want you to love me and to not have any doubts* and were this a few years ago you would have followed it with *Is that so much to ask*, but you're getting older now and you know that, in fact, it is. *I can't do that* she says and you say *I know, I'm just telling you what I want.* She says *I want to be able to doubt and not feel like a villain*, and she twiddles a faux-villainous mustache above her mouth and holds her coffee mug like a martini, pets an invisible cat. *I want you to trust that I'm a grown-up now* you say and she says *I want you to be a grown-up now* and you say *I can do that*, and she says *I can, too*, and as you shake on it you think *If I get any more grown up at this point I'll hang myself. It's depressing*,

.   .   .

Two years ago you stood in a room full of boxes, wondering when she'd acquired so much stuff, and how she'd managed to fit it all in your tiny shithole apartment. She asked whether you wanted to keep any of her books because they were too heavy to move, and you said *No because* and the end of the sentence was obviously *they'll remind me of you* but instead you said *I've read them all.* Her phone rang, then, and to her credit she tried to let it go to voicemail, but in a weak moment you picked it up from the nightstand and saw his name on the screen, said *Go ahead, answer it* and her eyes said *You sure?* and you said *Whatever, you're his problem now*, which you didn't mean, only said it because it had been so long since you'd been in a position to hurt her, and now again you were. You wanted to provoke her, wanted her to fight back because arguing was the only language you knew anymore, and even if she said something nasty, at least she'd be speaking to you. She took the phone from your outstretched hand and said *This'll just be a minute* and walked outside, closing the door before you could slam it. You locked her out—a pointless gesture, you knew she still had her key—but before you could even enjoy the temporary fuck-you of her trying the knob and noticing you'd done it, you heard the engine of her car start, the wheels crunching over pebbles as she backed out and drove unceremoniously, and irreversibly, away.

.   .   .

You've reached a point in the conversation where you both feel comfortable sitting in silence for a bit. She leafs through her book but doesn't give it her full attention, just spreads out the pages like a Japanese fan. Whoever the middle-aged man has been waiting for still hasn't shown up, but someone's dog wanders over to his table, and when he notices it, the man smiles. The dog nuzzles his hand and the man is happy to pet it, happy to scratch its neck, happy to give it love. Something childlike enters into this man's eyes and you want to point him out to her, to say *Hey check it out* and nod in his direction, but you don't want the guy to feel like he's an exhibit in a zoo, so you just stay quiet. He breaks off a piece of bacon from his sandwich and holds it out for the dog to take. Just as the dog starts chewing, a woman behind him screams *Baxter! Baxter get over here* and marches over to leash Baxter up, then turns to the man and says *Please don't feed my dog* and returns to her table before he can say *I'm sorry.*

.   .   .

One year ago you'd stopped speaking completely. Everything in the world felt so slippery, like walking through quicksand, that you took comfort in anything concrete, so you detailed your life in numbers: six nights a week getting sloppy-drunk, five drinks a night at least, four months since your last sober message on her voicemail, three months since your last drunken one, two packs of cigarettes a day, one girl a week you took home with you. The girls were the hardest statistic to keep track of, since they weren't really different girls so much as a poorly-constructed mosaic making up scraps of her. A waitress with a beauty mark in the same spot next to her nose. A blonde with the same cat-green eyes. An undergrad wearing the blue sweater she'd had on when you first met. In your defense, it was getting easier not to think of her while you were in bed with these girls, and you'd even taken two or three of them on a few dates. You brought one home to meet your ma and your ma said *I like her, a local girl* and you said *Ma please* and she said *I'm just saying this one's good, it's important to know your place.* But during all of this, you didn't kid yourself to think that anything was more than a distraction, a way to cope—*but what's wrong with that,* you thought—and it was impossible not to realize she was probably doing the exact same thing at that moment, you had no idea whether she was still with him (but what difference did that make?), and when one of these girls laid you down in your drunken stupor and put a cold washcloth to your head and told you it was nice to take care of you, you felt so profoundly lonely that it was all you could do to keep from throwing up.

.   .   .

Are we just lonely she asks you, and for the first time in the negotiating process she's thrown something at you for which you weren't prepared, because honestly *Yes* is the answer—*but what's wrong with that,* you think. People get together for much worse reasons. But she says it again, aims the question for some reason at the back cover of Didion's book, at a sad-eyed black-and-white picture of the widowed author's face, *Are we just so lonely that we're coming back to each other to get rid of it? Are we that fucked up?* And you go *No* and look behind you before you realize that you're the one who said it. But it's true, *No* you say again, *I could be just as happy by myself. I don't need to be with anyone.* And she says *Seriously* and you go *Yeah* and she goes *Well then what's the point* and you let that sit, stir the coffee with your pinkie, take out a cigarette but leave it unlit, roll it back and forth on the table like a kid making a snake out of Play-Doh. *It's true that I'd rather be with you than be alone* you concede, *but I'd rather be alone than be with anyone who isn't you,* and you say it not romantically but matter-of-factly, because it is a fact, a truth, probably the only true thing you know anymore at a time in your life when all the things you used to think were true are proving so oppressively false. And maybe she picks up on this truth-vibe, because she says *Okay, say the worst thing you've done to me that I don't know about,* and you say *No way am I falling for that,* and she says *Come on, come on* and you say *No* and she says *Do it* and you say *I have no idea if*

I ever loved you, and she says *I cheated on you* and you say *I thought it had to be something I didn't know about,* and she looks down and says, L*ots of times.* But this does not stun you in the way it would have when you were younger, this does not break your heart or even mildly sprain it; it occurs to you that you actually *meant* the thing about not wanting to be with anyone who isn't her, and you do after all love her and this (cheating) is after all what people do and you are after all just a poor boy from a poor town, living a life that until she showed up felt impoverished itself, so instead you just say *I want you to stop doing that.* She says *Okay* and *I want you to stop drinking,* and you say *Well—we can talk about that.*

.   .   .

One week ago she called, *Just to say hi.* You'd never been call-just-to-say-hi friends, or friends at all for that matter, but you were so grateful to hear her voice that you didn't question it. She said she'd been thinking of you often lately and you said *What about...* and she said *No, he's gone* and you said *Why* and she said *You.* You didn't know whether their break-up had made her think of you or her thinking of you had broken them up, and this seemed an important distinction. But you got to talking casually and it was nice; you'd spent so much time trying to remember what she looked like that you'd forgotten to remember this, the most important thing, the ease with which you spoke to each other, the only-her things she manages to say. *I wish we'd known each other when we were kids* she said and you said *You wouldn't have liked me, I was weird* and she said *Me too!* which actually you knew already, she'd told you about the league of American Girl dolls she'd gather in her attic and boss around like an empress; you'd told her about the broken fridge in the alley behind your house you used to crawl into and sleep in to feel somehow less lonely. But you were talking again now and that's what counted, that's what made this all feel new, that's what made you agree to meet a week later and see *how* and how *much* and *whether* you'd changed, the answer being *Not much,* which is why, a year from now, you'll be standing in a room full of boxes again, she'll be driving unceremoniously away, this time for good.

.   .   .

But for now you are here and she is here and peace talks are going well, and you have to admit you can't remember ever feeling quite as happy as you do now, when she brushes back her hair, smiles at you, and says, *Well hello there stranger.*

Ted McLoof teaches fiction at the University of Arizona. He writes about characters suffering from arrested development, usually while they watch Arrested Development and listen to Arrested Development. His work has appeared or is forthcoming in *Minnesota Review, Bellevue Literary Review, Monkeybicycle, Hobart, DIAGRAM, Kenyon Review, The Rumpus, Louisville Review, Ninth Letter, Los Angeles Review,* and elsewhere. He's been nominated for a Best of the Net Award. *ANHEDONIA* is his first collection.

www.ingramcontent.com/pod-product-compliance
Lightning Source LLC
Chambersburg PA
CBHW020239030726
47497CB00009B/3175